Hiawatha Passing

BY **JEFF HAGEN**

PAINTINGS BY **KENNETH SHUE**

HENRY HOLT AND COMPANY · NEW YORK

On a cold starry night, a boy awoke in the upper reaches of his grandparents' tin-roofed farmhouse. Only moments before he'd fallen asleep, his harmonica at his side. Now he thought he'd heard a low, distant sound. Did it come from outside? He snuggled beneath his feather quilt, trying to figure it out.

This was the first time he'd spent the night at his grandparents' place, nestled way out in a land of rolling hills and faded red barns. Far below his window two silver rails stretched across a wide valley covered with a thin layer of new snow.

What was that sound? he wondered. It had come to him as a soft hum, like a gentle breath on his harmonica. *Was it a dream?* He listened. Nothing.

Slowly he rolled to one side of the bed and blew a puff of warm air onto the window, melting a little spot on the frozen glass. He pressed his finger there, rubbing away the frost until he created a porthole. Then he peered deeply through the hole, like a pirate squinting into a spyglass, searching for mystery ships in the night.

For an instant the boy caught sight of a glint on the frozen steel railroad tracks at the edge of the farmyard.

Now he heard it.

A high-pitched whistle cracked across the countryside like the snap of a bullwhip. The rails began to hum. He could almost imagine them turning color: changing from cold lifeless black to brilliant flame orange, throbbing with energy and promise.

Something big was approaching the farmhouse.

A single light shot through the darkness.

He could see a dark shadow behind it, swaying back and forth, spraying snow as it plowed down the valley.

The light thundered by the farmhouse, leading a huge steam engine. The earth trembled. The house shook.

A string of box-shaped lights flew by, roaring and rattling.

Within each box was a blurred face peering out into the night: framed pictures of midnight travelers.

Who are these people? the boy wondered. *Where are they going? Why aren't they asleep under their feather quilts?*

Suddenly the last car whooshed by, its red taillight becoming smaller and smaller in the distance.

Little frost crystals spun and danced like toy tops until they came to rest on the frozen ground along the silver tracks. Silence returned to the valley.

The boy took one last look at the fleeting train, and at that instant a shooting star etched a brilliant trail across the velvet black sky.

Sleep overcame the boy. He was lucky; he was content. For on this night, at Grandma and Grandpa's farm, he had witnessed the passage of two shooting stars, one on earth and one in the heavens.

Hiawatha, 1935–1970

In 1935 the Milwaukee Railroad System introduced a new train on its Chicago-to-Minneapolis run. Faster and more powerful than other trains of its day, it was considered to be in a class by itself. The train was called the *Hiawatha* and was nicknamed the "Fleetfooted Indian." Within two months of its inaugural run, the *Hiawatha* gained international fame when it became the fastest train in the world, surpassing the record held by an engine on Great Britain's London and North Eastern Railway. For the next two years the *Hiawatha* continued to set both speed and ticket-sale records.

During the 1936 season, the *Hiawatha* consistently attained speeds of 100 m.p.h. over sustained distances on its routes through Minnesota, Wisconsin, and northern Illinois. Its fastest recorded speed was 112 m.p.h., between Watertown and New Lisbon, Wisconsin.

Federal speed regulations curtailed the competition between American and English trains in the late 1930s. The *Hiawatha* went on to become one of the legendary trains of all time, carrying millions of people across the heartland—until 1970, when the southbound "highstepping" *Hiawatha* made its final journey through the valleys and ridges of Wisconsin's driftless land and slipped off into history.

I grew up in a hundred-year-old farmhouse in southern Minnesota that overlooked a valley where the night trains passed. Every Christmas, I rode the *Hiawatha* with my family from Minneapolis to Chicago. Forty years later, the excitement and wonder of that childhood experience is a crystal, enduring memory. My story of the *Hiawatha* is dedicated to my son, Kit, and to all those who have ever listened with their heart to the long, melodic call of a locomotive engine passing in the night.

—J.H.

To my son, Jonathan—K.S.

Henry Holt and Company, Inc. / *Publishers since 1866*
115 West 18th Street / New York, New York 10011

Henry Holt is a registered trademark of Henry Holt and Company, Inc.
Text copyright © 1995 by Jeff Hagen
Illustrations copyright © 1995 by Kenneth Shue.
All rights reserved.
Published in Canada by Fitzhenry & Whiteside Ltd.,
195 Allstate Parkway, Markham, Ontario L3R 4T8.

Library of Congress Cataloging-in-Publication Data
Hagen, Jeff. Hiawatha passing by Jeff Hagen: paintings by Kenneth Shue.
Summary: While sleeping at his grandparents' farm one winter night, a boy is awakened by the mysterious and powerful sound of the world's fastest locomotive passing in the night.
[1. Hiawatha (Express train)—Fiction. 2. Railroads—Trains— Fiction.] I. Shue, Kenneth, ill. II. Title.
P2Z.I11235Hi 1995 [E]—dc20 95-6067 / ISBN 0-8050-1832-8 / First Edition—1995
Printed in the United States of America on acid-free paper. ∞
10 9 8 7 6 5 4 3 2 1
The artist used oil paints on canvas to create the illustrations for this book.